The Adventures of Pajama Girl

and the Coronation of the Cupcake Queen

"Thou shalt not steal."
Exodus 20:15

by Sandra Hagee Parker

Illustrations by Sarah Bussey

WORTHY®
kids

Hi! I'm Ellie, but you can call me Pajama Girl.
This is my little sister, and I call her Sis,
but she prefers to be called Princess Sis . . .

Every morning for me starts the same way—
pancakes, school and then home to play.

But when my chores and school work are finally done,
that is when my fun has just begun!

Every night I look forward to bed because
I can't wait for the adventures that lie ahead.

It is my pjs that are special, you see,
for whatever is on them will be in my dreams.

If I'm in the mood for a tropical breeze,
my palm tree pajamas are all that I need.

Or maybe I wish to travel way up high –then my hot air balloon footies will take me up in the sky!

But tonight I'm in the mood for something sweet,
so these cupcake pajamas will make the perfect treat.

Time to pray!

"Thank You, God, for this day,
and thank You for the special way
You've blessed me and Sis and those we love
with all your blessings from above.
And now as we lay down to sleep,
we ask that You give us dreams so sweet."

I open my eyes and can't believe
what is in front of me . . .
it is a kingdom of cupcakes,
as far as the eye can see!

As Sis and I walk down frosted streets,
we start to sample the delicious treats.

Everyone is preparing for a huge celebration! One of the villagers tells us, "Today is the Cupcake Queen's Coronation!"

We make our way to the castle
and watch with wide eyes,
as the crowds line up
to see the parade go by.

Arriving at the castle gate we are surprised, to see
the most beautiful queen with the saddest of eyes.

I say to Sis, "Go play, go explore.
So I can talk to the queen and
see what all her sadness is for."

"Oh Cupcake Queen," I say, "will you tell me please
why you are feeling this way?"

The queen turns and cries, "Today is my party,
my coronation you see, but this cupcake celebration is not
meant to be! For someone has stolen every sprinkle in sight,
and cupcakes without sprinkles just isn't right!"

"Cupcake Queen, please don't you worry;
I will find the sprinkles, and I'll be back in a hurry!"

I searched high . . .

And I searched low, but not a sprinkle
was found. I searched high in the heavens . . .
I crawled down on the ground.

I looked and looked, then thought of something
I missed! Two heads are better than one;
I must search with my sis!

I called out her name, "Sis, where are you?" She said,
"I'm over here; I'm playing with someone new!"

I came upon the most unbelievable sight!
It was Sis jumping into a pool of sprinkles,
her laugh filled with delight!

"Where did you find these sprinkles?" I exclaimed.
"I've been searching all over, but not one remained!"

"Ellie, you told me to go off and play, so I met
a princess and we've had such fun all day!"

"She has a pool of sprinkles you see, and we've been practicing our princess cannonballs. It's as fun as can be!"

"Tell me, Princess, why do you have all of these sprinkles? Don't you know stealing from others is bad?"

"I stole them from Cupcake Kingdom," she said. "I stole them because I was sad."

"A coronation for the Cupcake Queen just cannot be, not without me! I was not asked to lead the parade, so I stole all of the sprinkles. There will be no party today."

Just when I thought there was no hope,
the Cupcake Queen pulled up
in her coronation float.

"Cupcake Princess, do not be sad. You were not asked
to lead, because I saved the best for last.
You shall sit on this float, and together we'll ride.
You will have the best view; you'll be right by my side."

Then the Cupcake Queen turned and exclaimed, "All of you shall be princesses; come ride in the parade!"

"The title of princess for me doesn't fit—just call me Pajama Girl, but you can call her Princess Sis."

So together we rode, down coronation mile.
There was waving and cheering and many bright smiles.

But the very best part came at the end
when sprinkles started raining down on our heads.

All was well in the Kingdom of Cupcakes and treats and the queen's coronation was a spectacular feat.

Then all of a sudden, out of nowhere,
a familiar smell began to fill the air.

The smell of pancakes and syrup opens my eyes,
and as I sit down to breakfast, I'm surprised to find
a reminder of my nighttime dreams,
is left in my pocket, where no one else sees.

"Mom, it's not Ellie; just call me Pajama Girl."